THE E

Lord and Lady Evil

Dr Y

They want to rule the galaxy.

THE GOODIES

Boo Hoo   Jet   Tip

They want to stop them.

10

There was a roar of engines.

Everyone looked up.

"Here come the baddies!" said Boo Hoo.

16

One of the Wees shook his head.

"Why did Lord Evil send *clowns*?"

"I think he meant to send *clones*,"
said Jet.

Dr Y's ray gun shrank the Wees.

"We've got to stop him," said Boo Hoo.

"Cover me!" shouted Jet.

She started to sneak behind Dr Y.

Easy!" said Boo Hoo. "Just like this!"

He pushed Tip.

Jet shook Dr Y's gun. "Oh no!

It's jammed..."